THE SNOWFLAKE MISTAKE

Lou Treleaven & Maddie Frost

High, very high, almost too high to see,
an ice palace floats like a ship on the sea,

Where clouds are collected before they float by
to make all the snowflakes that fall from the sky.

SQUISH

goes the roller to squash
the cloud thin.

CRUNCH

goes the puncher to stamp the flakes in.

"I want them all perfect!"
commands the Snow Queen.
"If any don't match, they're not fit to be seen!"

But young Princess Ellie would much rather play
and chase all her friends in the sky every day.

It's fun with the birds choosing storm clouds to ride or whizzing along down the big rainbow slide.

One morning the queen has some business to do,
appointing an artist to paint the sky blue.
She calls the princess, "You must mind the machine.
Make sure the flakes match. It's your turn to be queen!"

"Goodbye!" calls out Ellie,
then runs off outside

to search for the birds
as they take turns to hide.

But all of a sudden the sun slips away.
The palace is cloaked in a cloud of cold grey.

"SNOW!"

shouts out Ellie with all of her might.

"We need to make snow!" But there's no-one in sight.
"What should I do? I'm supposed to be queen!
I'll use DOUBLE SPEED on the snowflake machine."

SNOW QUEEN

SPLAT

goes the roller to mash
the cloud thin.

CRASH

goes the puncher to bash the flakes in.

BOING goes a spring.

There's a **BANG**!

And a **POP**!

And everything comes to a horrible stop.

Ellie climbs up the tower
to view the sad scene.
Where white was expected
there are still fields of green.

No snowballs are flying. No snowmen stand tall.

No sledges are sliding. It's no fun at all.

Poor Ellie stares down at the far-below land,
then jumps up with joy. "I can make them by hand!
I'll cut up some clouds - they'll be different, I know,
but no-one will mind just so long as there's snow."

Snip snip go her scissors.
"This job will take weeks!"

The birds flutter in and peck
shapes with their beaks.

Soon snowflakes pile up.
Some are big, some are small.
"They're perfect," says Ellie,
"Let's scatter them all."

The hills become white like a pile of iced buns.
The children catch flakes on their noses and tongues.

The rooftops are tucked into spotless white sheets and snowmen stand proudly on driveways and streets.

The queen comes back home.
Snowflakes rest in her hand.
"These all look so different.
I don't understand."

"I'm sorry," says Ellie, "I made a mistake.

I broke the machine, so we handmade each flake.

They're all different sizes but nobody minds.

They love having snowflakes, whatever the kind."

The Snow Queen peers down at the scene far below.
"I've never seen anything quite like this snow.

Each flake is unique in its own special way,
but seen all at once, it's a dazzling display."

She hugs Ellie proudly. "You've been very clever.
I love the new flakes. It's the best snowfall ever!"

High, very high, almost too high to see,
an ice palace floats like a ship on the sea,

Where a queen and her daughter make snowflakes together to throw from the sky in the cold winter weather.

The End

Make a Snowflake

You will need...
- A square bit of paper
- Scissors

1. Get a square piece of paper (you could decorate this with glitter!).

2. Fold the square diagonally in half.

3. Fold your triangle in half again, across the diagonal.

4. Fold paper in thirds. One corner to the front, the other to the back.

5. Trim the extra piece of paper off the end of your small triangle.

6. Cut lots of shapes around your triangle.

7. Open it up and you have a snowflake!

1.

2.

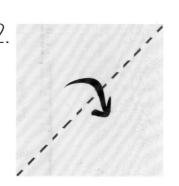

3.

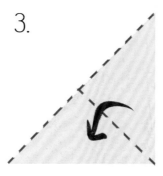

7.

4.

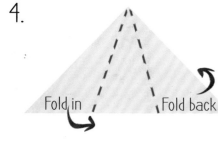

Fold in   Fold back

5.

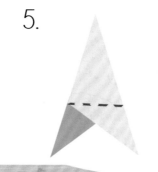

6.

The Snowflake Mistake
is an original concept by
© Lou Treleaven

Illustrator: Maddie Frost
Represented by Bright Illustration

A CIP catalogue record for this book is available at the British Library.

Published by MAVERICK ARTS PUBLISHING LTD

Studio 3A, City Business Centre, 6 Brighton Road, Horsham, West Sussex, RH13 5BB
© Maverick Arts Publishing Limited September 2016
+44 (0)1403 256941

ISBN 978-1-84886-218-0

Maverick arts publishing